THE WORD

A Bedside Reader for Insomniacs

George A. Sivore

authorHOUSE®

AuthorHouse™
1663 Liberty Drive, Suite 200
Bloomington, IN 47403
www.authorhouse.com
Phone: 1-800-839-8640

First published by AuthorHouse

7/30/2008

ISBN: 978-1-4343-9212-1 (sc)

Printed in the United States of America
Bloomington, Indiana

This book is printed on acid-free paper.

To Katy,
My life,
My love

Remembering...

Steve Allen, NBC
Richard Kiley, Man of La Mancha
Robert Jamplis
Mike McDonnell

OUR DAILY BREAD

Whatever happened to Bread? To our plain old Loaf of Bread? Check your friendly grocer's shelves, you'll see. Nowadays there is no such thing as "A" Loaf of Bread. Now shelves are loaded, -besides white, and rye and wheat. In fact, some stores have their own ovens to bake it on site. To keep up with our preferences. Fresh. Personalized. Their problem is giving the same dough new shapes and tastes. –And names.

Poor ole' Bread. It seems to be suffering the same fate as much of our complicated lives. We're not satisfied unless we have more and more choices. Look at today's array. Cute names like Cobblestone, Soft Oatmeal, Country Buttermilk. For the body-builders, Branola, Nature's Own, Hearty Choice. You want nuts? How's Oat Nut, Date Nut or, you guessed it, Health Nut (no pun).

And then there's Bread named after romantic places, like Vienna, White Mountain, Bahama. As the man says, if we ever have a Bread Crisis, it won't be because of new recipes or baking ovens. We'll just be running out of names to call it –or places to name it after.

Hey, here's another one. It's, Lifestyle Italian. Wow! Now that's for me. In fact, that IS me. I've always dreamed of lolling on The Riviera. Me and my Katrina over there. In our cozy Cabana, playing my accordion. Sand in my shoes. A little Chianti. Munching on a slice. Ain't mad at nobody.

O SOLE MIO ♫ ♫

CONTRIBUTIONS aka OUR THROW-AWAY SOCIETY

This whizzing-by world of ours. We stroll on the Moon, phone from the car, E-mail our Cousin in Lisbon. Most everything is old hat. Change. In fact as my friend is wont to say, Life IS change.

A classic example of this lifestyle just popped out of the mouth of our Grandson. Seeing Dad puttering under the hood of their VW Bus, the four-year-old blurted, "Why fix, Daddy? Buy new one."

And isn't that just about it. Our modern ways. Our attitude today. Fortified by gizmos with questionable lives. Mass produced in some far-off Land. Maybe that's the point. Throwaways we toss away when they quit working. Or we tire of them. Or their usefulness. The labor to repair that electronic marvel costs more than buying another. Much more. I gotta tell you, it's a whole new ball game.

Look around the house. Go no further. Once upon a time, if your appliance went on the blink, which was rare, there was Mr. Fix-It, in a store down the street. He had the parts to revive it because it came from Kenosha or Syracuse. But not now. Our guy, Mr. Fix-it, couldn't make a decent buck anymore. So he gathered up his tools and flew south. Retired.

Who closed him down? No, not some Mafia Bad Guy in a black hat and dark glasses. It was a Sweet Little Lady. You don't know her. Probably somebody's mother. And she didn't waltz in and take over his store. Heck, no. She's still back in Taiwan or Guatemala or Singapore, knocking out TV's and transistors all day and slurping guacamole and rice-a-roni at night. She's good at her job. Mostly, she's cheap.

And speaking of our Foreign Friend, the Somebody's Mother, -she might have even made your FAX machine. But she doesn't have one. So if yours goes bonkers, don't try to FAX her up and ask her what to do about yours. Or where to take it. No way. Relax, Chester. It's The System. Toss it. Drive down to the store. BUY NEW ONE.

* * *

EPILOGUE

If all these happenings get you feeling kind of sad 'n dumpy, sitting there in cold an' snowy Chicago, you can always fire off a postcard to your pal, Mr. Fix-It. Maybe brighten the dismal day. you can catch him on the beach, down in Florida.

Just say, "Wish you wee here".

I GAVE AT THE OFFICE

I don't know about you, but I'm getting swamped with letters and phone calls these days asking for money. Soliciting. And all because of electronic mailing and phone machines, making it easy to reach me. They buy lists of names, push buttons and my phone rings or my name shoots out on an envelope. I'm fair game. Nailed. In fact, if they don't leave me alone, pretty soon I'll be on the Endangered Species List.

Everyone wants a piece of me. And not only the old Causes, like Dimes, Cancer, Red Cross. There's a whole new bunch of Appeals out there now, cutting in on these venerable folks. Heartrending pleas. Babies Without Milk. Adopt A Highway. Homeless Wild Animals. Food for the Elephants. So many Celebrities clamoring to sponsor a Cause, it's getting hard for some Stars to find a nice disease not already taken, an ailment they can feel comfortable with.

The past Holidays were typical, a windfall for fund-raisers. Like everyone, I got my share. And in The Spirit, I caved. Now, a while later, I'm getting thank-you notes. Wow! I'm euphoric. To think these busy folk would take the time to acknowledge my little check. But, whoa! Not so fast, George. Nestled in with their thank-you note is

ANOTHER envelope. Just In case I want to send them more money. I'm crushed. I should have known better.

I tell you this asking for money business has become so big, most Causes hire professionals to raise the dough for them. Many states even have Gift-Givers Guides. Like a phone book. Thousands of names. Charities. Causes. What they take in. And it's not uncommon for some Groups to keep as much as HALF of what they collect. Imagine!

Here's one. I just head from some Guys in Washington with a great Cause, Save The American Farm. Their mailer pictures a bunch of Cows mooing, "Join The Herd". So I "mooed" back, - Money. Though I know all about Swifty's in Las Vegas BETTING the Farm, I never heard of SAVING one. I'm curious. Gotta' take a flyer on this one, frolic with Guernsey and Herefords See, I'm from the City, but I always had a patriotic feeling for Moms and Apple Pie and Red Barns. –Wanta' be a COW-boy.

Washington calls it SOFT MONEY. I'd add, 'from SOFT GEORGE.

GREETING CARDS

Boy, am I gonna' catch a lot of flack for this one! Talking about Cards. Greeting Cards. Remembering Loved Ones on that special occasion with a fancy card you just picked up at the store. It has somebody else's picture, another guy's words. You only buy it, sign it, and lick the stamp. It's not a very personal message. Maybe a little lazy.

I know, I'm treading on shaky ground. Because thinking of a Dear One with a nice Card on their Big Day is admirable. As they say, it's the thought. It's Sweet. Traditional. American as apple pie. Everybody likes the idea. Witness the companies producing 'em by the millions. And they ain't cheap, Buster. Big bucks. A huge industry like U.S. Steel and General Motors. Except without smoke stacks.

But what I've gotta' wonder is WHY? Why all the fuss and bother? Sending Cousin Paula a card that's got a pretty picture and some soupy lines that rhyme. Instead of a thought or two of our own. Not that I wish to disturb our fragile Economy, but sometime, just every once in a while, why not?

In fact, I have an idea. The next time you're browsing the card racks in your market, how about choosing one of their plain cards, with nothing on it. Not even a cute Puppy Dog or Dutch Windmills. And then YOU scrawl your own words.

Write something like, "I miss being with you today". Or, "I won't tell anyone you're having ANOTHER birthday". Maybe "you don't look very sick to me". Throw in a couple of big X's, for kisses. Or say, "I'm too darn cheap to buy you an expensive card. Get well soon. Love ya', your Nephew, Joe".

Yeah, try that last line on your rich Uncle Tim's card. He might like seeing you being frugal for a change. Could forget they call you the Big Spender. Even smile your way, think it's a funny line. Put you back in "The Will". WOW!

Come to think, I could use that message myself.

HOORAY FOR TUESDAY

Poor Tuesday. Like the comic said, "it ain't got no respect." It's kinda' like the poor relation of days. Nothing happens. In fact, some Tuesdays get to be so dull, you just feel like standing around and doing nothing, waiting for it to go by. Not that anybody's especially mad at it, but worse, nobody remembers it. When it was? Where you were? Or if it rained? If you get where I'm coming from. And if you asked most folk they don't even have an opinion on Tuesday, either way. They can hate Monday and love Friday. But Tuesday, it's sort of a shrug your shoulders, "ugh" day. It just happens to be there, and nobody can do much about it.

Take the mail. You tear open bunches on Monday, big time. 'Cause everyone got rid of it on Friday. But nobody gets Good mail on Tuesday, since it would have to be sent on Monday. And who's in the mood for licking stamps and pasting envelopes after those Huge Weekends, let 'lone going to the Post Office and standing in line. Of course, what throws my theory out of whack are the big Ed McMahon Contest jobbies, wanting to mail me a million bucks. I get those on Tuesdays. But, as I say, nothing much interesting comes.

In fact, when you get to thinking, it's just that Tuesday is this nobody-cares-about-me day. You wonder if some

Calendar Guys ever said, “Hey, let’s print a new kind, and leave out Tuesday. – Jump right from Monday to Wednesday”. It’d sure save a lot of space and money. And you wonder if anybody’d protest, or maybe even notice. ‘Specially if it don’t goof up The Tides, or bother The Vernal Equinox, -what’s the diff?

Here we got Friday, which is so popular they’re even naming Bars after it. –AND celebrating and singing because of. ‘AND thanking God for. Then, of course, we all know about those Lazy Saturdays and Sundays. When even The Lord says you should only pray, and play golf on.

And lately, Monday’s been getting a lot of flak and heat, for being sad and gloomy. So they call it a Holiday every once in a while and close the Banks. Just to make it glad and let everybody feel better. Which only leaves the other two days to figure out what to do with. Our Guy, Wednesday who has a “D” in his name that nobody knows what to do with and Thirsty Thursday who gets a free pass, ‘cause he’s so close to his cousin, Happy Friday.

So now we’re back around to my friend, Poor Tuesday. The Nothin’ Day. And since I told you where I’m coming FROM, lemme’ explain where I’m going TO. I wanta’ make Tuesday a SOMETHING Day. Make it one of those days folks get all excited about. “Boy oh boy, I can’t wait ‘til BIG TUESDAY rolls around”! Yeah, I know I’m bitin’ off a large morsel. I know it’s a stretch. But I think I can swing it.

Here's the deal:

Based on our well known and very popular Law of Life:

> Nobody ever likes –or wants to, bounce out of bed on Monday. So why won't we all feel even better lolling in the sack on Tuesday? TOO? In fact, maybe more so.

Like after Holiday Monday we could throw in Holiday Tuesday. For MORE fun. Since everyone loves to get things free, why not give another day? At least do it once in a while. Then we'd only have those Wednesdays and Thursdays to worry about, before starting our big Party-Party Weekends. Again! So what's wrong with that? For one thing, I'm sure we'd be wearin' out a heckuva' lot more mattresses and Lazy Boys. And everybody knows that'd boost the Gross National Product. –Which is good.

Think about it.

IT COSTS MORE

Today, Friends, let us delve into another segment of our Super Market food products. Not an earth-shaking subject, but certain bothersome. For some of us, one of life's little compelling questions. It's the age-old phrase, "if it costs more, it must be better". How many times have we heard it, said it ourselves? But is it always true? Well, instead of dancing around the subject, I decided to find out myself.

In this case, the topic was Butter. Brands. Quality. Cost. Isn't all Butter the same? It's all AA Grade. Is there really a difference? There sure is in the price. And what was my problem. Why should I pay more for Brand A, when I can buy the Market's Brand B for a lot less? As I say, it was compelling. I had to try. I wanted to become an authority.

So I bought a pound of the two Butters. And one bright sunny morning, I did it. Taking time off from a rather busy Retiree's Schedule, I conducted my very own, one-man Poll. My own taste-test. I spread half a slice of warm toast with Brand A, the other with B, and asked myself the question.

My less-than-scientific test result: confusion, a fizzle. I was out of my league. Maybe it was just too early in the morning. Whatever. My discerning taste buds had failed me. I actually liked BOTH. I got so much joy, just tasting my samples, I forgot which was A, which B. Much less which was the better butter. And, come to think, I hadn't even considered Oleo.

* * *

EPILOGUE

Last week, the expensive Brand A was on sale. So I bought, not one, but TWO packages to "save money". I must confess, I'm a born snob. I'm not about to argue, fight City Hall. I figure if it costs more it MUST be better.

Besides, I'm sick of polls.

A FRIEND'S WATCH

My friend recently received a gift. A handsome wristwatch, with silver and gold link band. Numbers, tiny dials, buttons. It can perform most any function, perhaps compass him home, should he be lost. But this automatic timepiece, doing so many things is not the point of my comment, as wondrous as they may be. I'm more concerned with today's jeweler and his ability to market a product so many people want to own. One that that seems to tell the world they've arrived. And curiously, the more features, the more little hands, dials and movements, the better. Whether the Guy/Gal wants, or really needs them. Hear me out.

First, let me say this commentary is the result of a recent Industry Poll of watch owners. It noted that an alarming rate of 92% of folk receiving a Scuba Watch for Christmas loved their gift, but were claustrophobic and did not Scuba. In fact, some feared water deeper than bathtub levels, not being able to swim. Worse, some New Yorkers couldn't spell "Scuba" without adding an R. And also very troubling was a survey footnote that many polled were unable to tell time without moving their lips, -at least not very good. And so I must conclude I'm on to another rock-solid position favoring Vouchers and School Choice. Do I digress?

Getting back on track, I'm also bothered by the fact that it is very difficult these days to find a watch with big hands, that simply tells the time of day. One that doesn't have the picture of a mouse on the face. Tough to find a watch even Guys with bad eyes can read. Oh, I imagine if I browsed the shops in Zurich I'd find many. But around here it isn't that easy. Most likely I'd see plenty of digital jobbies reminding me of my dashboard kilometers. I do have problems.

Of course I must admit these new watches are very popular. And if one happens to have a strong wrist, that doesn't tire by five o'clock, and no history of arthritis in the family, it's not my worry whether you Scuber, -or even spell good.

Except, one other thing. If you do receive one of these gems you should see your Tailor. Pronto! Ask that he shorten your sleeve a few inches, to better show off your nifty new gift. Then you can have that classy look, without appearing pushy.

NAILS 101
(a Saga)

"Beware of product in a plastic package, it cost's more". An old Tibetan Proverb, learned well at my Mother's knee.

Sadly, I found the fact, first hand. So true. It's not enough to have a great product anymore, you've got to have it "Packaged", to make it sell. Wrapped, boxed, labeled, maybe a little plastic window. Colorful. Never mind that when you get it home you trash the wrapper. For some wild reason, they tell Charlie, the guy behind the counter, that his gizmo sells better if it's in a Package. A pretty Package. So now we got this whole new Industry out there, like US Steel and Boeing, wrapping products in plastic. And that's OK, if they want to play games with me. It only gets bothersome when it causes a direct hit on my lifestyle.

This one happened a short while ago, on a beautiful Spring morning. A morning full of promise. When I decided to test my ole' handyman touch. It was a simple chore, hanging a favorite picture on our wall. It only required three things, A Hammer. A Nail. And Me. And I already had two parts of the equation. However, since I was nailless, a visit to my friendly hardware store was in order. I needed "A" nail.

There, at the store, I got my first lesson. There I learned that in this day of strolling on the moon, cell phones and e-mail, there is no such thing, anymore, as "A" nail. Today, sadly, to get "A" nail, you must purchase twenty – in a plastic package. Twenty nails to get one. It's some theory concerning the Laws of Economics and John Maynard Keynes, -and more jobs. No matter. Trust me. It's The Law!

Long gone is the hardware store with bins in the aisle, full of all kinds of nails. If you needed one or two, they were there for the taking. Grab yourself a hands-full. No charge. Charlie would say "catch ya' next time". Nowadays we have racks. Display cards. Bright packets. Windows full of nails. Beckoning. When all I wanted was one. Fact is, you can't buy "one" of anything, anymore. Because they don't have the nerve to charge you for "A" screw or "A" tack. And believe me, they DO want to charge you. Even if it's only a few pennies.

Besides their accountant would go nutty over my sale, deciding if he should enter it in his ledger as Petty Cash or Petty Nails. So now I'm buying this whole package of twenty just to get me my one little nail. Believe me, it doesn't exactly make my morning.

Concluding my Picture Project, I must admit it was a rousing success. In fact, my wife called it a great show of my talent and engineering skills. It did, however, create a sore and tender subject: my final ignominy. I'm now confronted with this package of nineteen extra, and useless, "A" nails, housed in an ugly, busted-open piece of plastic.

The plan was to store them in my sock drawer, where they could be easily found. (A secure repository for valuables, my Will, Passport, Important Papers.) If it could just be re-sealed and not mingle with my sweaters 'n socks. It was troubling. And all the while I kept thinking of that Guy in a black hat and dark glasses, who started the whole Industry. Who actually got paid to dream-up my goofy plastic package for nails. Just so the Kid at the hardware, Charlie III, (the one in the Reeboks and the lab coat with his name), could dump twenty nails on me. When I only needed one.

I tell you, such things shouldn't happen to a very nice fellow, on a beautiful Spring morning.

* * *

EPILOGUE

Later, slouched in my Lazy-Boy, I'm pondering. My picture's on the wall. A sticky Band-Aid, is soothing my pinkie. I'm happy. Still I have myself this sock-drawer, with little nails strewn around. When, even with luck, I figure to only need another one or two before next Thanksgiving. So guess where my devious mind is taking me?

Would you just happen to know of anyone in the market for a bunch of pre-owned "A" nails? –In a torn open plastic package? My socks would be eternally grateful.

THINK ABOUT IT

Our Joe has a great line. Whenever he's back into a corner. Whenever he's unable to sell his idea, his suggestion, he backs off with the line, "Well, -think about it".

It's a great approach, -either way. For you the promoter, or you the pigeon. On either side of the fence, the phrase can be very apropos. It's so classic. Yet sometimes neglected and maybe deserving of a little comment.

Consider, how many times we wished we'd have taken the advice ourselves? To, Think About It? To go easy, slow? To hesitate, wait a minute? How many dreams, plans, decisions have we made that didn't turn out so well? When waiting a bit longer wouldn't have been such a bad idea? To, Think About It? It could be endless.

In business, buying a house, marriage. Whatever. A lot can be said for the phrase. Not to say all our rash commitments are wrong, 'far from it. And adding this boy-girl to the equation may cause some flak. However, how many beautiful lives could have been saved, had we put things on "hold" for the moment. To have backed up from the trees, viewed the forest? How many moments in business have we rushed to rash conclusions? Then second-guessed ourselves over an impulsive decision? We were anxious. Greedy. We didn't take the time to, -Think About It?

As we look back through our young lives, there aren't too many times when it wouldn't have been a bad idea to slow the pace a bit. Too many times when, for the want of a minute, a day,- even longer, that a push on the Ole' Pause Button may not have been the better, the best approach.

In fact, Omar, maybe YOU should heed the advice. Consider your new investment. Don't mean to run your railroad or flog the horse. But do you really want that "water-front" bungalow down in Alabama? Even if it is a steal.

Thank About It.

OUR NUMBERS GAME

The other day I got to thinking about Numbers. That there are different kinds. In fact, I went a little "scientif-tic", and decided by my count, there are three kinds. Like All Gaul, Numbers are divided into 3 parts: 'ZACT, KINDA' CLOSE & BALL PARK. We use them in different ways. In fact, live and die by all three. Lemme' explain.

The first kind, 'ZACT, we don't play around with or ever forget. Like our Social Security Number, our Bank Balance, rich Uncle Tim's Birthday. We can't mess with them. They gotta' be on the money. 'ZACT. And if you don't believe it, try sneaking another zero onto your financial statement, and see just how friendly your Friendly Banker can be. Or hit a six instead of a seven on that long distance call. You could wind up talking "surf" with some bronze beach boy out in Hawaii. Any way you look, you're in deep trouble if you mess around with 'ZACT Numbers.

Then there's the KINDA' CLOSE Version. The ones you can fudge, or shade a little to make you feel good. Like your age. The size of that Sailfish you almost caught. Bragging about your golf game or running the table at Vegas. They don't hurt anybody, and still make you feel like the Big Sport you are.

Finally there's my favorite Numbers, BALL-PARK. Them babies are mostly huge ones, don't take a lot of "brainer" to remember and are bound to liven your conversations. Actually BALL-PARK are the oldest kind of Numbers. They come from the Greek word, Ballparkus, go way back to those ancient Olympics, written in stone.

Back then, Pizza Vendors had a way of casin' Rome's Coliseum Crowd. Times when The Guys in string sandals, head-bands and lumpy togas were pushing pepperoni pies, BALL PARK'n the house so they didn't run out of cheese. They're that old. (And if you were good in Latin Class I wouldn't have to be explainin' all this).

Anyway, you get the picture. Our Numbers Game. Take your pick. Hang on to all three. See which one's fly at your next party. Throw around some BALL PARK's, -the World Debt, Size of Siberia, How High's the Moon. It'll show folk how smart you are with Numbers.

Just one word. Don't get yourself too deep into the pizza story, especially with that Cute Doll sitting over there in the corner. She may not share your enthusiasm for mixin' anchovies and Ancient History. Might tell you to, "cool it, Charlie".

THE BOX

Fortunately or unfortunately, for better, for worse. Our modern everyday lives are inescapably governed by our appliances. Our Gizmo's Electric. The TV's, the phones, kitchen aids, computers, even things that we still crank. True Creatures of Our Century. Happy and loving most moments of a convenience-made existence.

Over this lap of comforting luxury, however, dark clouds hover. Like termites, most every home is infested. Every home has lot's, commonly referred to as "The Box". An empty box stuffed with wrappings, odd Styrofoam shapes, sticky tape, how-to-use directions, in three languages. Once they belonged to a grill, a blender, a recorder. Now they're piled in the garage, the attic, under beds, wherever. Gathering dust. And we plead guilty as charged, descendants of an old Roman Tribe, Amigos d'Box. (Friends of The Box). In short, if it came in a Box, anything this side of a Honda, it's fair game. It has a home. In our home.

But why? Why are we all victims of this phobia for saving boxes? Simple. It's our psyche, waiting-for-the-other-shoe-to-drop Syndrome. Terror-stricken that if our purchase ever goes wacky, if one tiny chip gets loose, we're in Big Trouble.

We all have vivid pictures of dear little ladies in Taiwan, sitting at tables, putting together transistors, cameras, calculators. Bunches all over the floor. So sometimes they just gotta' have bad days, get mad, kick a couple, snap a wire. Bust one. (Maybe after a cold Rice-A-Roni lunch). But if we get that lemon, happen to wind up with a bum one, we can always take it back, if –we got The Box. Anytime. Without The Box, we're dead!

Seems The Box is more important than The Gizmo. Might even cost more. No matter. That darn Box is the key. If we got troubles, no prob. Forget warranties, serial numbers, dates. Just dig out the Ole Box, pack it up and get on down to the store. Tell the guy, man to man, "My wife told me to bring it back. It's here. It don't work". And he says, "Piece a cake, Pal. I see you got 'The Box'. Grab a new one off the shelf. And have a nice day."

Voila! I'm saved! – To battle The System, yet another day.

* * *

EPILOGUE

"Now let's see, Joey's baby-bottle warmer, he'll be seven in July. Where-in-heck did we put The Box....?"

WE'RE OFF & RUNNING

This week has certainly been eventful. It can, I believe, be termed the "Pre-Owned Week" in our young life. As the result, we are Off & Running, with a happy new attitude. And all, mind you, because of our newly acquired possessions. Both equally important. Both, to use the term of our times, "Pre-Owned". They are a reconditioned garbage container, (can, if you may) and a beautiful, late-model automobile. It's a long story. Let me explain.

The former, The Can, happened this strange way. As a result of our newly automated City Sanitation System, the garbage pick-up is now a one-man operation. A truck driver controls the pick-up from his cab command-post. Driving up to The Can at our curb, he presses buttons, clamps on to the can and upends the contents into his truck. Then, after a big of Shake and Shimmy he sets the container down and takes off. Mission accomplished. Neatly done. No hands. Only, on this bright and beautiful Saturday, the S & S part of his operation went awry. He did such a thorough job, he also shook loose – and swallowed – the lid. Our abode became a Top-less Can residence. Subject to wind, rain, storm, animal and pestilence. We needed a new top. But quickly.

Now, as you probably are aware, there are few things in life as significant and concerning as garbage. Envision a load strewn about your beautiful lawn. Try some coffee grounds, egg shells, banana peels, booze bottles and chicken bones from a Midnight Raccoon Picnic and you readily get the picture, you will understand our plight. So, it is of utmost importance that, while in one's yard, the container be neatly sealed. –which is where the lid comes in.

In any event, and not wishing to flog the horse, a top-less trash can is no cause for happiness. Conversely, a new fully-operational can, with closing lid, is reason for joy. Albeit pre-owned and refurbished.

Re the second topic, acquiring our Pre-owned automobile in this same hectic week was equally joyous. Incidentally, in these provoking times, no one terms such transactions as buying a Used Car. Horrors! Today one acquires a Pre-owned Sedan. It lends a classier tone (like our Grandfather's Clock). Even pictures the Sporting Man in Touring Cap, Goggles and Gloves. One who may have paid more than intended, but was not "taken" by his salesman. No matter. One possesses a beautiful car. More importantly, it is paid for.

Concluding this early morning scene, we are both proud and pleased with our newly acquired, Pre-owned Pleasures. In fact, as we ponder our bucolic and stately Manor Setting, we view a spiffy Gaar-bage (French) Container in our back yard. And an elegant, low mileage Motor Car gracing our circular drive. Contentment abounds. There is no doubting. Life is good. We're movin' on up.

THOSE CELL PHONES

A while back I thought I was right up to speed with a few thoughts on Beepers, those tiny communications boxes. The Second Cousins to our telephones everyone is wearing to "stay in touch". The ones that Beep when someone is hot on your trail. I thought I was with it, making small talk, mentioning that so many of our citizenry proudly display their Beeper boxes-on-belts as a status symbol. Some, even if they don't work or have a battery.

Well now, before I lose any more sleep on the Beeper, I'm confronting an even bigger scourge, the Cellular Telephone. The Cell to you. The pocket size phone to call anyone, anytime, from anywhere you are. Walk down the avenue, visit the market, ride an elevator. Look and listen to people using their Cell. It's our latest toy. In fact, drive down the highway, see the folk whizzing by, one hand on the wheel, one on their Cell. At the rate we're going, Cells may soon be standard on cars as bumpers and head lights.

You have to wonder, is the Cell releasing some new torrent of our pent-up words? Can people have more to say now, than a while back when there were no Cells? I see Guys and Gals backing out of their driveways, -gabbing on

Cells. Are we in that much of a hurry? Wouldn't it have been easier to make the Call from their breakfast nook, or have waited 'til they hit the office? More importantly, who's keeping an eye on the road? The driver ahead?

Worse, MADD –Mothers Against Drunk Drivers is REALLY mad now The AAA says the Cell won the honors, took over top spot. The Cell Phone replaced MADD as #1 cause of auto accidents.

I'm telling you, you can't please everyone these days, no matter how hard you try.

THE WORLD'S RICHEST LADY

Friends, I would like to introduce you to a very nice Lady. A very busy Lady. And, because she happens to be so busy, she's become the Richest Lady In the World. Actually, a few years ago, she was just Somebody's Mother, barely getting by on her Social Security. Today, she's a very Famous Inventor. And, more than that, a Lady of untold wealth. Her name is Hilda Glockenspiel. This is her story.

First, about her Invention. Well, it's not that she really build something like Henry Ford putting a crank and a gallon of gas on his horse-less carriage. Or young Tommy Edison building 'n busting light bulbs out in his garage. Her thing has to do with words. And, I know, you can't patent "A" word But Hilda invented SIX words. She put them together and snuck her idea thru the U.S. Patent Office one day, when all The Guys were busy eating lunch and playing football cards. Now anyone who says these words on the telephone has to pay Hilda a royalty. Because the words belong to her.

The words she thought up, that she invented, are: "YOUR CALL IS IMPORTANT TO US". The next time you phone some big company and they are busy, instead of hanging up on you, and making you mad, they flip on Hilda's Words. 'And she gets a penny. (Two penny's, if they say the words in Spanish, -and call you Amigo).

Now maybe this doesn't sound like big bucks to you, Armando. But just think, -the number of times you've made a call to a business, expecting to talk to a real live person. To hear a friendly "Hello", or "How's your weather down there?" And all you get are Hilda's Words. Over and over. YOUR CALL IS IMPORTANT TO US. It's crazy. And now everybody's using them. In fact, even my plumber, Irving, -when he and his Stilson Wrench happen to be laying under some guys kitchen sink. They sound so homey 'n nice. Even if they truly ain't either.

Best of all, Hilda found this loop-hole in the Tax Code, The Piggy-bank Proviso. It's got something to do with the IRS being too darn busy chasing down Big Shooters, to be bothered snooping around, looking for People's Pennies. –At least, not THIS year.

OUR WAY WITH WORDS

Welcome to our World of Words. To the latest trend toward playing with Words to doll up our Lifestyle. Words for any and all occasions. Maybe a little deceptive word to throw us off the track. Call them cute. More Attractive. Salable. Be it a phrase on a product, to catch the eye of the buyer, the title on a man's card to make him sound more important. This Game with Words.

Check the ads in your newspaper, you'll get the picture. Honest Abe is still pushing his Used Cars. But now instead of USED Cars, he presents them as PRE-OWNED. And he never SELLS them. He OFFERS them with his Tail-Light Guarantee, (good so long as you're in sight of his lot).

Then there are the Banks, famous (or notorious) for titles. That Man greeting you at the front desk is Vice-President. Perhaps a Third or Fourth V.P. But, hey, what's a number, it's a title, Bank Vice-President Which is almost as good as a raise. And over there is the head honcho, pardon Managing Executive.

Come to think, this tossing Titles around is not confined to the Business World. Churches are into the act too. The Convent, former home of our Sisters, is no longer. Oh, the residence still stands, but with the Dear Nuns long gone, the sign over the door reads: Religion Resources Center. Our beloved School Yard is now called The Campus and the Pastor's new assistant has become a Parochial Vicar. My, my.

Incidentally, don't you worry about our Men of Medicine. They are also in this Words Game. Witness their new terms. Some time ago they quit doing Operations. Today they confine their practice to Procedures. They perform PROCEDURES. And tho, I admit, it does sound much nicer and a little less painful, I still receive the same Bill, 'er Statement for SERVICES.

And so it goes, in this wacky World of Words. Actually, I could go on, but Katy just handed me a big chore. You see, we have a lot of junk in our garage. She wants me to haul it to The Dump. Only thing, where do I go? Where is it located? The City Dump closed. Say, wait a minute, they did just open a LAND-FILL.

I wonder, is that the same old Dump with a fancy new name? It seems to have a familiar scent and I do recognize some of the flies. Are the City Fathers busy sprucing it up, trying to make it a nice place to visit? Especially when we tire of going to The Shore for our picnics?

Say Katy, we could bring our chairs and the beach umbrella.

A WORD ON HOT DOGS

In our never-ending pursuit of a more prefect world, we continue to complicate the uncomplicated. Keep making trouble for ourselves. Adding confusion to our already too-organized lifestyles. Like asking for problems when there are no problems. Muddying our water.

Take, for instance our beloved Hot Dogs. Next to Apple Pie and Cheeseburgers, they're runner-up All-Americans. They have everybody's vote. But now Madison Avenue is getting into the act. Not content to let these beauties be just ordinary Hot Dogs, our advertising friends are coming up with fancy names and new tastes. Tinkering to make them a little ritzy. Trying to sell us on something we don't want. As the man says, "If it ain't broke, don't fix it."

At the stadiums, we just yell to the vendor, "gimme' a dog". Nowadays at the market it's not that easy. There's decisions to be made, because the shelves are loaded with them. All kinds. Instead of picking' up a package as you and your cart roll by, you've got to think. Do I want the Bun Size? Fat Free? the Juicy Jumbo? the No Salt? Maybe I should try a package of Diet Dogs?

Yesterday I asked The Man, "don't they make my plain ole' Hot Dogs anymore? I can't find them in the case."

His answer: "yeah, we still carry 'em, but we just sold out again. How about tryin' our new Teeny-Weenie Weenies. We got lots of those."

MY NEW WATCH

I just bought a new watch. No glitzy silver and gold timepiece to impress my friends, still the purchase has given me a thrill and exhilaration beyond words. Man! I'm in Hog Heaven!

What, in the past, may have been termed a timepiece, well this one is something special. Not only does it tell me the time of day to the second in my home, but, at the very moment, in London and Hong Kong (which some day could come in handy). And it also performs many other functions. Like it can run with me, swim with me, even compass me home should I get lost. So many, many things. In fact I have ten tiny pages of features (and instructions) to brighten my life. Everything, except the name and phone number of an understanding psychiatrist, should I find the urgency. I may.

In an earlier life I had what they called an Alarm Watch. I could not only tell time, at which I became most proficient, but I could set the dial to make the alarm go off, even when I didn't want it to, (like in Church). It was an excellent helpmate. I loved it dearly. So much so that I gave it to our First-born Son, Tony. Which day I later came to regret. But that's another story.

Fast forwarding to the present, I have for months sought a similar timepiece. It has not been easy. Because there is no such thing as a wristwatch, nowadays, that simply tells you the time and beeps like an alarm on request. To obtain only these functions you must buy a watch that lights up, provides the date and perhaps the depth of your scuba dive, in meters. Even if you can't swim, or care to Scuba, you get the feature. It's truly interesting concept, says Chauncey, my garage mechanic. Again I digress.

Let's just say that I now have this handsome watch –and ten pages of instructions on Chinese rice paper. When all I really wanted was a watch that would tell the time and "alarm" me, if properly set. What I didn't take the time to reason was that we now happen to be living in the 21st Century, and nothing is easy. In fact, Our Fathers, have devised ways to complicate even the most mundane habits in our daily life. But, there I go again. Suffice it to say, this watch is not what I really wanted. Yet this is what I got. So, in the likely event I can save even one poor soul from my fate, I will continue to preach my Gospel, like Saint Paul. Believe me, with this purchase I have opened myself a very nice can of worms. Big time can. Huge worms.

Specifically, these directions. They contain words like Mode. Analog. Countdown. Timer. Start/Split. Truly the only feature that I readily understand is the section adjusting the watch band to fit my wrist. And these instructions, I see they're only in English, nary a gesundheit to help my German Friend, Hugo, who just put down a bunch of Marks for one of these babies in Berlin.

And I think I got troubles?

* * *

EPILOGUE

Some months later, and since penning this elegant and incisive tome, I, unhappily, must report no progress, learning to operate my new Watch. Yes, since you asked, it fits my wrist beautifully. Thanks to my ability to master details. But that is the only thing I'm good at. I still don't know how to make my alarm, alarm. Nor do I understand, or see reason for, the five buttons on the side. I do believe one, or two work if I'm big on the Stop Watch feature, and wish to clock myself jogging down to my mailbox. And I'm also fairly certain one button illuminates the dial. Because I bumped it yesterday and my wrist glowed like it was in the x-ray machine at the airport. (It didn't hurt). But that's my limit.

I asked Lopez, my Cuban Jeweler, for clues in operating the device. Sadly, he just shrugs his shoulders and mutters something in his native tongue, ending with "Amigo". So I assume he still wants to be my friend and take my money, -if nothing else. Yet, even in Spanish, I detect he, too, is on shaky ground.

Steadfastly refusing to heed his unintelligible words, leaves us in this Mexican Standoff. And the only reason I report the matter in the first place, is that down deep I truly have a feeling of envy. A feeling that this little timepiece is part of a whole new age of wonderful and enchanting electronic wizardry that lies before me. If only I would take the time, have the patience to –"R the D's".

As my Dear Mom, Alice, was wont to say, "What's a Mother to do"?

PANTS
A CRITIQUE

Thru the Centuries, our Ancient History Books have recorded many chapters on The Rise and Fall of the Roman Empire. It's one of the staples of our studies. However, no history lesson today, Students. We're not talking Peoples, we're talking Pants. THEIR popularity. THEIR Rise and Fall. That's right, the kind You Guys tug on every morning, one leg at a time. Something we dare not leave home without. And, as such, this critical cover in our wardrobe seems worthy of comment. Because Pants, of late, have come on hard times. You ask the question, are they still loved? Appreciated? EVEN required?

Take my case. Just lately I showed interest in buying a new Tuxedo, only to find our men's stores are now selling the Pants SEPARATELY from the Jackets. Like they're really not all that necessary, not for everyone. Now, admittedly, Pants are not pretty things. But they are functional. They do serve a useful purpose. And the very thought that maybe, just maybe, one might venture out some evening in his spiffy new Tuxedo Jacket without your Pants spells heresy. Should Pants ever fall from favor, horrors!

If this bit of fashion-folly should ever become the rage in Formal Attire, who knows where it will end? If that Eligible Bachelor appears at the Debutante Ball in top hat and tails, stylish boxers and button spats, -but sans Pants? It could cause comment. Raise a few eye-brows. In fact, one wonders if even the sight of his colorful Kilts, and perhaps a plaid Cummerbund, would lessen the moment.

Further, should Pants ever veer toward extinction, like the Edsel, the Water Buffalo and the Hula Hoop, we envision our Department of State AND the British Foreign Office, noting the crisis “grave”. Because, for one thing, they have these huge inventories of striped trousers in storage all over the World. Lend Lease. At the ready, for any and all Affairs. Surely a drop in the “P M” (Pants Market) would arouse those Geezers at the International Monetary Fund. May even concern Our Guys keeping an eye on The Yen.

So much for Pants, the FALL. Now to study Pants, the RISE.

We should begin my mentioning that Man’s Pants, like Fido, his Puppy-dog, have been a Best Friend thru the Pages of History. Endorsed by World Leaders, the Religious, the Bon Vivant. In fact we note, Pants have been a hot ticket ever since Learned Man gave up on lacy cassocks and lumpy togas. And they probably peaked in popularity in the last Century. That is when the well known Hungarian Tailor and Dandy, Hyman Lifschultz, came to America with his famed invention, The Two-Pants Suit.

Hy's U.S. Patent #72317, virtually eliminated trousers wear and tear. (They took twice as long to wear out the seats.) It was truly a boon to sitting mankind, wearing Pants. At the very least, extra Pants were seen as the Equestrian's Answer, as they pranced along the garden paths, -bouncing up and down in their saddles.

You see with Hy's Invention, a gentleman received two pairs of Pants with his new suit, for the price of one. His slogan "More Pants – Less Shine", shook the Nation. Every man's closet became loaded with extra Pants, -that didn't shine. Pants were "in". Then later, the moment was only dimmed when the noted Italian Scientist, Guglielmo Marconi, stunned the World Scene with his Invention of the Wireless Radio. And tho Hy never won the Nobel Prize, as did Guglie, there's still a School that believe Hy's Invention more important. Fact is, when you see half of the world walking around with some on, they do have a good point.

In any event, it is safe to say that Pants have long been popular. So long, in fact, that even the name, Pants, began to wear thin. (No pun). Then Washington got wind of the story and wrote their famous Pants Proviso, -giving Pants dignity and a new name. They were no longer to be called Pants, they became Slacks. This sounded more classy, and expensive. And, for a kicker, Congress added a sneaky Midnight Clause giving ladies the right to wear them. Too. Before many men got wind of the new Law. It turned out to be a real vote-getter. Popular. Passed without filibuster.

Ladies loved the new Bill. In fact many of the Fair Sex thought it was as important a measure as Suffrage and the Auto Act, giving them the right to drive a car. And jog, outdoors in bikinis. (A distraction frowned on by the AAA.) However, ladies never did take to Hy's Two-Pants idea. Probably because not too many of them ride horses to work. And besides, they never have enough space for extra Pants in their dressing rooms. No matter. Pants became the "latest" for ladies, as well as gentlemen, with their cognac and cigars. It was a fashionable trend at the Old Guard Party's de rigueur.

Then came another devastating blow to Hy and his Two-Pants Invention. Besides Marconi stealing his thunder, the Tuxedo Tailors of America (TTOA) came up with a real money-maker. They decided to sell their Tuxedo Suits a new way. So much for the Jackets, so much for the Pants, pardon, Slacks.

Now, today, we find the Industry making Business Suits studying this loophole. If they should ever decide to sell their Pants as an extra –and charge more, it might spell trouble. Spell the demise of trousers, as we know them. A Pants Revolution could be looming. And we all remember the ill-fated Knickers Crash of '47, when Men quit wearing "Plus 4's". Just imagine, from TWO-Pants Suits to NO-Pants Suits. And all happening in Our Lifetime. Sad.

Happily, for now, Pants are still popular with Wall Street and the Upper Crust. Yet there's still this nagging move toward those cute Bermuda Shorts and Argyle Knee-Socks on Fridays. When it isn't snowing. Except, of course, for the Amish riding around in their quaint buggy's and black hats, in any kind of weather. Besides, men will really get mad if they have to pay extra for Suits with Pants. When they could be using the money for betting on football pools at the office. And going to hockey games with The Boys.

In any event, it may be a nasty trend. One worth watching. One that makes some of us a tad uncomfortable. The thought that we'd ever be receiving invitations to The Gala reading:

"Black Tie. Pants Optional". (and embossed)

* * *

Ed Note: There is a tad of truth in this tome. Actually was a Clothier on State Street, Chicago, who sold suits with two pair of pants, -for price of one. No, his name was not Hyman. And that ends our little bit of whimsy. Period. Paragraph.

JACK STANTON, was as dear a Friend as a Guy could have. And I was privileged to call him just that, My Friend. As such, he was also the butt of many of my Funny Lines.

A “straight man”, if there ever was one. This following incident, a typical evening classic.

I truly miss the Guy.

DINNER AT EIGHT

Many nights Katy and I, living close by The Stantons, would share our Martini Hour, -solve the World’s Problems. It was a home and home series, if you will. Visiting their abode, we always sat in their cute breakfast nook off the kitchen. Invariably Dorothy’s organized dinner entree would be sitting on top of the stove, ready to pop in the oven. Our reminder that it was not protocol to dawdle over ‘teenie’s beyond six o’clock, The Stanton’s Dinner Hour. We went along with the Dear One’s schedule.

One such evening, with great flourish, Jack put on his best quizzical look, asking: “Dorothy, why can’t we have dinner a little later some night, like Katy and George? Why do we always eat early, -with the Bo-hunks?” It was a funny line, and just for our benefit. Tho Dorothy didn’t see the humor. Nevertheless, this was her ritual. Once she had her second “cap-full” of Scotch, dinner was in the oven. We always took the hint. We vacated the scene.

In any event, it was my opening for another "Jack" Story. So one evening, returning from Stanton's, I staged my very own "photo-op". Placing some colorful paper napkins on our kitchen floor, I added a candle, a wine goblet, and a rose. Then, into this stately setting, I plopped our cat, Monster, with his big bowl of Fancy Feast. It made for a stylish, kitty din-din. A moment that needed to be recorded. And so it was. Monster gobbling away in elegance. By candlelight.

Later, I gave the photo to Jack, titled: "Dinner at Eight".

His classic reaction, waving the photo, -typical Stanton-ese.

"See Dorothy, even Sivore's Cat eats later than we do".

STALLS & SPINS

In honor of the fifty-something anniversary of World War II, I'm reminded of times when I learned to fly in the Air Force. There was one training maneuver that always bothered me. My Stalls and Spins. I still shudder to think of it. Hear me out.

It happened in my earlier days, after a bunch of tests to qualify to be a pilot. I could have become a Bombardier, like my big buddy, Roy Sykora. He wanted action. A linebacker at Michigan, he was assigned to the 8th Air Force in England, flying bombing runs into the German Steel Curtain within months. His name is inscribed on a huge Wall in our American Cemetery in Holland. God Bless Him.

Back on me, I wanted to be a "pee-lot", (our French name). And having passed the exams, I became an Air Cadet. Proud of the title, my wings. Superiors telling us we were the cream of the crop. Future heroes of Our Country. Then came the hard part, in particular for me. The Stalls and Spins. It was one I couldn't buy. That one still makes me quake. For me, an Old Man of 26 years, I told myself: "George, you should know better".

The scene, the famed Thunderbird Field in Arizona, where they had just made a movie about flight training.

Our flying machines, a squadron of Stearman's, two-wing open cockpit craft. And we came equipped. Flight suit, goggles, helmets, gloves, and parachutes we sat on, -the whole nine yards. (I still remember lugging my chute home on leave one time, all the way to Chicago, if you please. Not to show off, but carrying that chute was my ticket to hitch a ride on any Air Force plane, going anywhere, any hour).

We took off twice a day, practicing take-offs, landings, dives (no loops). It was fun. Flitting around in the air, -like little birds in the desert sky. –Real live Snoopy's with goggles, if I may. In training but still able to enjoy the lesson. Far from War, with beautiful Camelback Mountain in the background. Not mad at nobody. And nobody mad enough to get on my tail, and shoot me down.

Then reality. To get more feel for our craft, we were given instructions in certain maneuvers; later told to go up and practice alone. Except one of these stunts was "Stalls and Spins". To me, this one was nutty acrobatics, and I didn't cherish the thought. I always had the queasy feeling it was the Air Corps way of wedding out the shy and timid. It usually did. In fact a member of our class panicked one day, he didn't pull up in time. There was an explosion, a puff of black smoke in the distance. It shook us. We lost a Cadet.

In any event, our orders for this stunt were to take off, fly up several thousand feet, cut power, pull back on the stick, easy-like, until the craft couldn't, -or wouldn't, climb anymore. It would stall. Silence for a second. Then the craft would shake, shudder, cough, whatever. And plunge, nose down. Me, my plane, My Maker. Gaining speed. A lot. Closer and Closer. Spinning. Down!

In these split moments I'd be picking out an object on the ground –like Farmer Jones' big red barn, -and count the number times I spun around His Residence. Faster and faster. Closer. Then, I was to kick in the left pedal, pull back on the stick and out of the tightening Spin. Smoothly, I think it said in the Manual.

"Boy, that'd be neat", you say. Some guys, the kids age 19, thought so, too. I was a vintage 26. I didn't. (It was like nothing I'd ever seen in my Ford coupe, -even on an icy Outer Drive in Chicago. The idea that I would deliberately put me and my plane into such an attitude, maybe get it mad, was beyond me. I had a crazy love of life. A joie de vie. Somehow I couldn't see Stalls and Spins a part of My Future. If The Air Force was to permit me to have one.

Too, I had this gut feeling that Farmer Jones, would become a bit miffed with me and my U.S. Air Force, if one morning he came out in his yard and found a big hole in his new barn. Look up, see me and my Stearman –goggles and all, sticking out of his hay loft.

But, not to worry. If it were me, I'd be real diplomatic. I had my greeting all practiced. I'd wave down to him, real friendly like, and shout:

"Oh, Hi, Mr. Jones. Sir. I don't believe we ever met".

HELP
A Senior's Lament

Help! We need Help! Assistance!

We are gradually becoming a Push Button Culture. No one talks. Everything we do in Communications, we say with Buttons. Whatever has happened to our precious Voice? Laryngitis is fast becoming as extinct as the Spotted Owl. Nobody gets sick from talking anymore. Because our Phone Buttons do all the talking for us.

Telephone a Business. Any big business. Even if only to ask their hours. A machine answers and puts YOU to work. What is your question? Who do you want to talk to? And for your every Button reply, you get another bunch of buttons to push. No more do you encounter a pleasant "Hello" or "Good Morning". No one asking, "may I help you?" Only a bothersome mechanical voice with her fistful of Button commands.

Actually, nowadays this whole Phone Button Thing puts the monkey on your back. It all happened because some Wise Guy sold big business on his idea. Buttons, he said, are the new thing, a heck of a lot cheaper to employ than People. Besides, they don't take coffee breaks or look for Social Security. Which all costs money. And isn't making money what our Grand 'n Glorious Country is all about?

Come to think, it's really very easy to figure. So why don't you just be a Nice Person, lower your blood pressure, and do what they say. Mind Your buttons.

Better still, get revenge. Hang Up!

Go fly your Flag!

IT'S A NEW ERA
A Senior's Lament (part 2)

It's the birth of a new Century. The 21st. Hoo-Ray! Hoo-Ray!

They tell me it's a time to celebrate. We made it. Well, lemme' tell you, Buster, I'm not joyous. In fact I haven't had my fill of the 20th Century, -yet. And all of a sudden I'm getting pushed into a new set of big numbers. Too much!

Oh, I can accept computer chips. And e-mail. And flying at the speed of sound. That's all progress. What's bothersome are these mechanical voices giving me orders over the telephone. It's the impersonal-ness, the cold-ness. The lack of a nice someone to talk to, to answer my questions. A real live Operator.

It happened again, just now. It's late on a Friday. The end of the day, end of the week. And I'm the proud possessor of a cute little red cellular telephone. Still I got huge troubles. No, not big troubles like the Gaza Strip, but to me, almost. Because I don't know how to operate the darn little phone, what buttons to push and when. And there's no real live person to confide in, to help me.

After "studying" the Directions, I've become quite adept at switching the tiny thing on, dialing a number and talking. That's all hunky-dory. I even know how to turn off my toy. But that's my limit. From then on I'm in the Twilight Zone. No way can I retrieve my Voice Mail, if someone calls and leaves a message. Or enjoy the other good stuff they tell about in the Book. And tho I read rather well, I'm no match for their graffiti of odd words and strange symbols. Worse, there's no living shoulder to cry on until Monday. Nothing to do but surrender to The System, hang up and head home. There to the cozy confines of my Katy and a Friendly Martini.

Mmmmm, them Active Ingredients, -they do solve so many of life's little indiscretions. Best of all, there are no "How To use" Directions on the bottle. None, really needed.

PUSHING ON A ROPE

Pushing on a Rope, an old, time-honored expression, is not very popular these days. But it could be due for a come-back. Pushing on a Rope. Impossible! Yet how many times do we fall into the same trap, attempt it? We can pull it. But push it, no way!

Translated, how often do we try to force the dreams in our lives? To maneuver a happy ending? Our ending? And how many times do we succeed? Rather, how many times are we foiled?

Pushing our Rope. We so desperately try. All we get is a wiggle. A twist. Bottom line. We cannot dictate, plan, direct our desires. Manufacture a future the way we want things to turn out. When will we learn? When will we realize we can only work hard, give it the full treatment, a go. Then back off. Let things take their course. Happen.

What a waste of time. Waste of energy. When we try to push that Rope, shape our dreams. Worry them through. Better we spend our time, once we've done all we can, best we erase the subject. Clear that Rope from our mind. Then we can better concentrate on our project of the moment.

Perhaps, another Rope.

LET'S NOT FORGET THE ICE

With all our tomes, I've never made much mention of ICE. Even I have neglected the subject. Yet it's a mainstay of our existence. Like my ole' buddies, "Salt" and "Tuesday", it ain't got no respect, no stature. Everybody's taking these Guys for granted. But, hey, they're important, great subjects, Pals. With Ice, being a particularly "hot" one. Not only in South Florida, but all around our world. In fact, I ask you Gomez, where would we be WITHOUT our Ice?

Just now, as I was busting open a bag from my favorite market, I got to thinking. There's a lot of be said for the substance. Like my store's Ice is COLD Ice. Small cubes, that don't freeze together or melt quickly, water down your beverage. Too, it makes for a great break-the-ice (no pun) intro at your next party. You can sidle up to that drop-dead willowy blonde over by the window, and start talkin' Ice. She's just gotta' think you're either a real Cool Cookie. –Or some kind of Weirdo Nut.

On a serious note, down here in the Southeast, a few years ago, we had ourselves a terrifying Hurricane, named Andrew. First of the season. Destruction. Suffering. Lives lost. Homes literally blown away. THEN, everyone noticed Ice. There was a run on it. Shortages. In fact, they couldn't produce enough locally. Had to bring it in from up North, for little ones formula, hospitals, hotels, food spoilage. Some, I remember, came from as far away as an ice plant in Michigan. Imagine the label, "Imported from Benton Harbor". Naturally, there was none to be had for general usage. You could be suspected of Communist Leanings, -if you ever even whispered you needed Ice to chill your cocktail.

Now, we're back living in happier times. With lots of Cold Ice. In fact, if you REALLY want to "cool it", there's a company in Norway that chops up 'bergs, 'sells Iceberg Ice. It has real snob appeal. In fact, the bag says it's "Endorsed by Ice Aficionados, -and Eskimos". Worldwide.

That, you gotta' admit, is one heckuva' frosty testimonial. A pleasantly chilling thought, -if one may bend a word.

OUR FABULOUS FAX

In these modern, whizzing-by-days of communications we have yet another marvel on our daily scene. It's the FAX Machine. And before it, too, will be replaced by e-mail and things even newer, let us speak in its behalf.

The FAX is, in a word, a kind of cousin to our telephone, except we write the words instead of talking them. And tho it's been with us for some years, around our house it's a new-found gem. Our toy for talking by writing, to anyone or everyone, worldwide. It's amazing how it has replaced the old methods of communicating. In business and now at home. No more can we use the tired excuse, "your order is in the mail". The FAX makes that document or letter as instant and valid as our phone call. In fact the only thing you can't get away with these days is FAXing a check to your Plumber. Tho you could give it a try.

Back on the miracle of the FAX in our private lives, it's entered ours in a curious way. For some days now, Katy and I have been planning a visit to see our kin, Betty and Ralph in Lisbon, Portugal. It's a beautiful time of year over there and our hosts made the "mistake" of extending an invitation, carte blanche. Now we're filling the air with FAX, "talking" over the Atlantic. And, FAXing our thoughts, seems to make them easier to understand than doing phone calls. No doubt less expensive, when you figure we always wind up discussing the weather, on the phone. In fact our holiday, our "Springtime in Europe", is just about set, thanks to the FAX.

Which brings to mind another FAX-advantage. It's about those nutty "Wish You Were Here" post cards, we send to friends back home, from our seaside cabana. (Usually the day before we return). By FAXing the thought, they receive it the very moment when we really are enjoying. It isn't that "Having A Wonderful Time" card they get in their mailbox, two weeks from Tuesday. When we're already back home. And I'm out in our driveway, -shoveling snow off the car.

DINING A LA GLITZ

Just recently Katy and I had the pleasure of going out for dinner. Dining rather elegantly, if you will. It was one of those trendy Florida spots. A Restaurant/Club on the top floor of one of our tall buildings. At dusk a breath-taking panorama. Tiny twinkling lights of The City beneath us. Red and white stripes of cars moving thru the streets. Truly a Christmas Fairy Land. A memorable sight.

Thru it all, and following a chilled Smirnoff-on-the-rocks, I found a little humor to add to the occasion. A Commentary of Our Times. Debunking these days of our life. The extent to which we go to impress each other. The Glitz.

This time it concerned the Menu we encountered. Seems the fancier the restaurant, the larger and heavier the menu. Leather encased, it's certainly no patsy for The Guy with an arthritic wrist. Beautifully done. Cute French phrases. In fact, one finds, the more French the stiffer the tab.

For added ambiance, we were given two Menus. (Captain dare not mix). Hubby receives the one with lotsa' dollar signs. Wifey sees no distasteful mention of money on her copy. None of those offensive figures after the entree.

Reason being, if she knew the cost of the Filet, our frugal Fair One might go el cheapo, opt for an order of Liver & Bacon.

Katy thinks the idea makes sense.

* * *

EPILOGUE

Incidentally, this Money-on-Menus custom is said to have begun back around the turn of the last Century. The opulent Gay 90's/Tiffany Lampshade era. When money was never discussed at the table, with the Elegant Ladies present. Only when the gentlemen retired to their drawing-room for brandy and cigars. Talked-about Times when The Great Gatsby and His Boys were buying banks and building railroads.

Sometimes I feel a little envy, -wistful for the picture.

PASS THE SALT, PLEASE

Poor ole' Salt. Everybody's pickin' on it these days.

After centuries of devotion to the dear flavor, lately some activists, looking for a Cause, decided on SALT. OUR Salt. THEY don't like it. Therefore, WE shouldn't like it. It's bad for us. If we use it, quit today! If we don't imbibe, don't begin the habit. It's "bad for you". And tell your Mother, too!

Typical. The angry, meddling times we live in seem to spawn these folk. Never mind that we have lived with Salt for generations. Loving it, enjoying its benefits. It was good for us. In the Air Force training, they gave us Salt Tablets after our work-outs. Mandatory, replacing body fluids. Now they have some "Study" WARNING against it. And here we go again, off on another wild ride.

No doubt, for some folk, Salt is not good. And if you pump enough into little Michael Mouse, it's curtains! But these crusaders are throwing the blanket on ALL of us. Us guys that thrive on the stuff. While enjoying the fruits of our toil, -spraying our steaks with Salt, they're calling Congress. Demonstrating. Working up Sam Citizen's blood pressure. The tail is wagging the Saint Bernard.

And now our grocery shelves are into the act, brimming with Salt-free labels. No-salt. Low salt. Kinda Like salt. Not one box saying LOADED with Salt for extra flavor. Added Salt for Joggers, Sassy Salt. Endorsed by Marathons. I tell you, it's a conspiracy.

Hear ye! Hear ye! Salt Lovers of America. Come out of the closet. Stand up, be counted. Make noise. Join the Cause. Brag out OUR SALT. Sing Salty Songs. Send Cousin Bob a big bag for Christmas. What we need is Organization. Get some big guys with good feet to carry signs. Find that Nut who says he puts Salt on his Salt.

Better still, get Washington to name a Secretary of Salt. Locate the genius who invented the stuff, Morton. Make him our Folk Hero. Stick his statue in the park, Saint Mort. For openers, track down the cute Kid on the Blue Box, -the one with the White Umbrella and the Mary Jane shoes. Yeah, that's the one, Little Susie Salt. Break out some flags. Call the Boy Scouts. Hire the school band. Susie to lead our Parade. She can spill Salt all the way down Main Street. Melt some ice, -if it's snowing.

ME AND MY BEEPER

Welcome to the world of The Beeper. The tiny electronic box. The telephone you don't talk to, or into, or listen to. The phone that does not ring. It "Beeps" when called, and shows the caller's number in a tiny window, Doctors, Realtors, even my Plumber, Igor, wear a Beeper. Next to the Cell Phone it's the communication's world marvel. Call them useful cute, fin-sy. Yes, they are all of the above. Plus another word. Sinister! You might say they're so good they've just about eliminated a cherished word from our dictionary. Privacy.

Some folk consider these boxes-on-your-belt a status symbol. They love them, wear them with pride. They have arrived. Then there's The Boss, "Beeping" his overdue salesman. And Wifey sitting out in the 'Burbs, zeroing in on her Harvey. It's their newest toy. In fact, a Guy is never very far from these predators when he's wearing his Beeper. He can't hide on his psychiatrist's couch, relax in some cozy Massage Parlor (licensed), even stroll down Bikini Beach. He's found.

The ominous Beeps can reach the most elusive Man-on-the-Lam. Hearing the sound tells him someone is prowling, a Nosy Nora is hot on his trail. A Beep-ER is tracking a Beep-EE. No longer can he say, "I was in Church", where there are no phones – even to Call Upstairs. (Thou Shalt Not Beep Your God, the 11th Commandment).

Love them, or cuss their sight, these devilish Little Boxes have become fixtures in our Modern World. I'm telling you, Omar, The Beeper is just the latest troubling member of Our Society. We're stuck with them. They are here to stay. And, for some of us, that ain't the most encouraging news.

* * *

EPILOGUE

Oops. Excuse me, I just got Beeped. Me, the Official Family Go-fer. And, this time it's not The Boss, or Wifey. Or a customer giving me an order. No such luck for me. It's Junior, Beeping me from school. He forgot his lunch.

Over and out.

LIFE IS WUNNERFUL

Life is "Wunnerful". Well, maybe not always. But, for many folk it is, -most all of the time.

Whether it's boosting their own morale, or just plain being built that way, whatever comes out of some people is great! Wonderful! Their glass is never half empty, it's always half full. The weather report is Partly Sunny, never Partly Cloudy. And isn't that a beautiful credo for living? To forever see the bright side of Life.

Don't get me wrong, I'm not complaining. In fact, just the opposite, I'm envious. Because, no matter the happening, the way things turn out, whatever. These people are always upbeat. And, you know, their mood is contagious. I'm even feeling better by the moment just penning this.

Take this morning, I had a call from Bob, the man who's cleaning our carpets. Only met him once, but he was on the horn just now, all happy and chipper. And asking how I was doing? Reading from his script, I said I, too, was feeling GREAT. And incidentally, hopeful that by the end of the day our carpet would feel the same. He thought it a funny line.

Envy, the word mentioned, is the answer. That was what I was feeling. I'll have to remember to practice that smile stuff a little more. Remind myself of what I have. Think of my God-given Health, Wife, Family. My Life. So the next time I'm dragging along in low gear, I'll pinch myself. Wake up! Jump-start my psyche into Fast Forward. VA, Va, Va, Voom!

Lawrence Welk, the pride of the Geriatrics, said it best. He made music, -and a small fortune, topping it off with his classic word to be remembered: "WUNNERFUL, WUNNERFUL".

BATTERIES

The other day I glanced down at my little desk clock. I surmised trouble. The hands told me it was 10:15 AM. Noting the sun was well along into it's afternoon glide, I wisely deducted something was amiss. Either the sun or my clock was "cuckoo". (No pun). And not wishing to delve into the wonders of astronomy and the sun's orbit, I took the easy course, deducted the problem must lie with my clock. Sure enough, my deduction was on the money. My clock's battery was not running. It was dead. I needed a new one.

Piece of cake, you say, but not so fast, Lester. Buying another 1.5 Volt battery, my tiny half-inch long power source, was not easy. At the store I saw displays bulging with batteries to operate everything from kid's toys to grandfather clocks, but none like mine. Then, when I did spot a 1.5 Volt, it was packaged with a second battery. (I was told it was fundamental economics. A tested theory that you must buy "TWO of, to get ONE of)".

Worse, the 1.5V two-package cards sit right next to an intriguing same-size battery in a single pack. In fact they look alike, measure the same. However, them babies make no mention of that magic "1.5V", -so obviously, they ain't gonna' work. I had to take that two-pack to get my battery. I did.

Now, back home, all is well. My clock and the sun are once again moving along in harmony, thank you. Yet I do have this nagging question. Outside of my purchase aiding our Gross National Product, what am I to with my spare 1.5V? Say, I have an idea, maybe I should save it until Easter, and give it to my Bunny? He could make his red eyes blink.

As the man says, it's a problem I don't deserve.

* * *

EPILOGUE

This story seems to grow better with age. Months later I'm in need of another AA Battery. At my super store, I'm told I'll find them in their Battery Center, aisle seven. Lo and behold they were, and on sale. But only in packages of eight EIGHT to get ONE. Modern day economics. Now, if only I had an electric train, a Grandfather Clock, a screw driver----.

OUR MAGNIFICENT MARTINI

"...and on The Seventh Day, GOD rested"

At the risk of heresy we must infer that after His Six Days of Labor, The Good Lord rested, surveyed his Work of Creation. Quite possibly toasting HIS Universe with the libation of the day. The libation that was to be, in later years, Our Heavenly Martini. HIS, perhaps a little heavier on the Vino of the Time. Nevertheless, a True Believer would not question that it was the very birth of Our Ageless Martini. To some historians, they are THAT old.

Matthew, Mark, Luke and John. Surely these Learned Men of the Cloth must have noted this moment on their scrolls. Yet not one picked up what was truly Divine Revelation. Nary a recorded mention of our Fine Friend in the Bible. Singular.

Now fast forward. Permit me, if you will, to hop-skip thru the annals of history. Delving BC to AD. More into AD. Whatever. We drift past Noah the Pyramids, the Crusades, Wars & Pestilence, -into the birth of the 20th Century. To visit our beloved Country of France. Peek in on Paris, the City of Light. It is here that we find our first flicker. Our first mention of this Eighth Wonder of the World. The Elegantly modern and cherished, Chilled Martini. Mmmmmmm.

Details of the scene are sketchy. Yet this much is written. It happened in the historic Hotel Ritz Bar, in Place Vendome A rainy afternoon. Harry, the bartender, was holding court, dispensing words of comfort and wisdom (in French), when a bedraggled, Wet and Weary Traveler staggered in. With his very life twisting in the balance, Harry seized the moment, provided our Samaritan with a chilled Gin Cocktail –straight up. Then, the coup-de-grace, a waft of Italian Dry Vermouth. Our W&WT sipped. Smiled. Within moments the transformation. Voila! From Depression to Exhilaration!

Born that very day, and forever known as a true and faithful friend, like "Pal", our puppy-dog. The Magnificent Martini.

Written in stone.

SONNY

In an earlier, less complicated life, I was proud to be employed by the Curtis Publishing Company of Philadelphia. The one founded by Ben Franklin in 1781. My first j ob. Eleven years old at the time, I sold magazines on Thursday afternoons after school. My customers, the folk at the suburban Illinois Central Railroad station, in South Shore, Chicago. It was a twenty minute trip for businessmen commuting from their day in town, returning from "The Loop".

My employer printed the popular weekly Saturday Evening Post In addition they printed the Ladies Home Journal and a farm publication. The Country Gentleman. I had my little canvas shoulder bag loaded with magazines, standing at the bottom of the station steps, getting in the way of weary business folk coming off the trains. It was a great location for hawking my mags, especially that Saturday Post.

The pay was minimal, but it was an adventure. And my real incentive was their book of prizes for sales. Bicycles, roller skates, bats, footballs, redeemable with colorful Greenies and Brownies Coupons. Call it a dream job, a first adventure into the "business" world. I was on my way.

Before proceeding, however, I must tell you about those other publications, the Ladies Home Journal and the not so popular Country Gentlemen. Them babies were tough to peddle in South Shore. And therein lies the "hook".

My coupon Greenie/Brownie pay for the popular Saturday Post was low. A couple of Greenies for everyone sold. The Ladies Journal was a little more rewarding. And selling a Country Gentleman was as good as moving twenty Posts. Gentlemen spelled a quick bicycle. Only trouble, the Journal and Gentlemen were much tougher to move in urban South Shore.

Take the Journal as a "for instance", you'll see my plight. In those Days of Yore, not too many ladies in our affluent area worked in the Loop. In fact, not too many worked. So it followed that not too many ladies got off my trains in the rush hour, to buy my Journals. And this "not too many" went right to my Greenie-Brownie coupon account. Or, didn't.

Truth is, my White Collar Yuppies of the day, coming off the "IC", never seemed eager to pick up ladies magazines like The Journal, -even to bring home to little wifey. This was a Man's World we're talking about. And any magazine that was big on pushing corsets and high button shoes, didn't have a heck of a lot of male appeal. (-An understatement).

It was the same with my Country Gentleman, but even worse.

This was a Farmers Magazine. Catering to men who liked to read about cows and goats and who enjoyed pictures of the latest McCormick Reaper. It had very little appeal to a man who spent his day trading stocks and bonds for a living.

In fact, my only sales were to some yea-hoo who thought my Country Gentlemen was about lolling on the beach at The Club They were never eager, or known to snatch up the next issue.

Of course, even Gentleman I coulda' sold like mad, outside the Feed Store, on the IC Station's rural Blue Island. But this was South Shore, white collar-ville, inhabited by Yuppies who only wanted my Post.

I quickly discovered they didn't have any burning desires to curl up for the night with The Country Gentleman. In fact, after a long day in The City, they didn't even care what Kid won the 4-H Contest, or the name of the lady who took the Blue Ribbon for the best 3-Bean Salad at the State Fair.

Winning my bicycle became a lost cause. Up in smoke went my Coupon Collection and my two-wheeler. Truth is, I didn't understand The System. I should have been satisfied to cash in my coupons in for a football or roller skates or baseball glove. Instead, I only wanted the grand prize. Only the unreachable Bicycle. I wasn't satisfied with any prize but the Big Tuna. As a result I didn't cash in on anything. I would up, stuck with nothing. Nothing but a drawer-full of Greenies and Brownies. The first sign of greed had gotten to young Sonny Sivore. Even at that age, it got to me, an experience never forgotten.

* * *

EPILOGUE

Looking back on that first employment, my view of the Business World was a wonderful experience. It taught me unforgettable lessons. Pride. Teamwork. Belonging.

I ask you, how many kids do ya' know who can ever say they worked for Ben Franklin? Even the company he founded.

And as far as that spiffy new red two-wheeler is concerned. Hey, no prob. Since my boss, Ben Franklin, never gave me one Ger, My Dear Dad, did. Come next Christmas Morning, he had one for me, there next to our big Tree in the living room. "To Sonny".

My only concern, we had a huge winter storm Christmas Eve. Christmas morning I awoke to four foot snowdrifts outside our apartment door. I was heartbroken, but I so-wanted to ride my bike that morning.

Have you ever tried carrying a brand new two-wheeler down three flights of apartments stairs? And then attempting to pedal thru the snowdrifts on Clyde Avenue, in a bitter cold early winter Chicago morning? I can tell you, it wasn't easy

Not even for a wildly excited, determined eleven year old.

MEMORIES OF A WAR

Memories of World War II. It seems to be the popular thing to resurrect those terrible days. And like the old sporting events that made history, everybody says they were there, living it first hand. The fact is, for WW II, most everybody our age WAS there. Guys enlisting, picking their branch of Service while they had the chance. An omnipresent Draft Board snaring anyone who didn't sign up. As the man says, I fought and fought, and I still hadda' go. Some Guys were "in" for more than five years. TWO Friends did not return!

In my case, I joined as an Air Cadet for Pilot training. Then after the Air Force taught me to fly, they had an over-supply of Pilots. Some of us went to Air Transport Command, managing their 10 ton priority Cargo. The supply wing of the Air Force, we flew The World in 4-engine, propeller planes. 190 mph, at 10,000 feet, in lumbering transports.

It was early aviation, requiring two ex-Airline Pilots, a Navigator, an Engineer, Radio Man and we Couriers. (All ex-Cadets, we said we were the sixth man in a five man Crew.) After schooling for the work, our class was split, half to a Base in Northern Maine for Atlantic flights, half to Karachi for the China-Burma-India Theater. I made the list that was sent to Maine. Thank God!

Taking off from our Presque Isle Base, we hop-scotched North Atlantic skies, day and night-long crossings. Newfoundland. Labrador. The awesome fjords of Greenland, Iceland and south to the tiny Azores Islands, 500 miles off Portugal. Then on to destinations in the U.K., Scotland and Wales, France or to North Africa's Casablanca. Wherever the cargo was destined. Even some runs into neutral Sweden. (we wore civilian clothes). Vivid Memories. So many Cultures.

One cargo I'll never forget, 40 yelping Alaskan Husky Dogs we picked up in Labrador and Greenland, for the Battle of Bulge in Belgium's snowy/slushy Ardennes Forest. Hitler's Pincer Drive to encircle Our Guys. It was a surprise! We threw all available bodies, including our Post Band, into this fight. Dog-Teams replacing bogged-down ambulances. Chaos! Wounded, legs frozen in water-proof boots. Charcoal limbs, unable to walk. Unexpected casualties. Horrible Mess. The Real Heroes! And all, just in the ending moments of these Long Years of Conflict.

Later, after celebrating those TWO Victory-Europe Days in the Deliriously-Wild City of Paris, our Maine Base was closed moved to California and Hawaii. There to join in the War with Japan, still in progress. Fortunately, that ended soon after those devastating Nagasaki and Hiroshima Atomic Bombs.

In these winding down, mop-up operations days, we flew 2400 miles to Hawaii, South to Australia or West to The Orient. Flying South we crossed the Equator to

Dutch Kwajalein, an atoll in the Marshall Islands, 200 miles below Hawaii, (the Hydrogen Test area). Then to the French colony, Noumea, New Caledonia, and finally flying 800 miles into Brisbane Australia.

Should the plane/cargo we were assigned be headed West-to-East, we crossed the International Date Line, on a flight to Guam. Then an 8-hour trip to Manila or North to Tokyo/Yokohama, Japan –in the shadow of beautiful snow-capped Mount Fuji. Sometimes it was on to Shanghai. We wore two watches to keep our records Local & GMT Greenwich Mean Time. (Re: Date Line, one year I had TWO Thanksgivings: in Guam, then flying East, a dinner in Hawaii.)

Most of our later Pacific duty, in fact, was more relaxed. The frightening Atom Bombs had sobered The World, They ended all conflict. Just clean-up work, Jap snipers tired in trees. It was over! We could return to our Loved Ones. The only question, how soon? Our True Heroes were discharged first, with the Guys who had never served overseas replacing them.

Later, I had the opportunity to take one more trip to Hawaii and Tokyo before Discharge, -at least return and pick up the laundry I left in Honolulu. But after all those Atlantic and Pacific crossings, -more than thousand Atlantic hours, I did not want to take a chance. The Good Lord had brought us through some tough situations, some scary times. I sure didn't want to "phone" Him again. Didn't want to be Wise Guy push my luck. Dismissed the thought. Stayed in California USA.

Besides, Leo White and I, and some others in our 1380th AAF Group, were awarded the Air Medal, -with our names engraved on back. Wow! We were ahead of the game. The Air Medal AND a Discharge!

Best of all, we would see no more WAR. No more living that c'est la vie, Point-of-No-Return Life. There would be no more of our "Tomorrow-we-die" flights.

Memories. Tragic, but beautiful Memories. An irreplaceable lifetime. Fast-paced, short-lived years. Thank you Lord.

www.ingramcontent.com/pod-product-compliance
Ingram Content Group UK Ltd.
Pitfield, Milton Keynes, MK11 3LW, UK
UKHW040019200726
13854UKWH00001B/274

9 781434 392121